PUFFIN BOOKS

Published by the Penguin Group
Penguin Books Ltd, 80 Strand, London WC2R 0RL, England
Penguin Putnam Inc., 375 Hudson Street, New York, New York 10014, USA
Penguin Books Australia Ltd, 250 Camberwell Road, Camberwell, Victoria 3124, Australia
Penguin Books Canada Ltd, 10 Alcorn Avenue, Toronto, Ontario, Canada M4V 3B2
Penguin Books India (P) Ltd, 11 Community Centre, Panchsheel Park, New Delhi – 110 017, India
Penguin Books (NZ) Ltd, Cnr Rosedale and Airborne Roads, Albany, Auckland, New Zealand
Penguin Books (South Africa) (Pty) Ltd, 24 Sturdee Avenue, Rosebank 2196, South Africa

Penguin Books Ltd, Registered Offices: 80 Strand, London WC2R 0RL, England

www.penguin.com

Angelina Ballerina first published by Aurum Press Ltd 1983;
published by Viking and in Puffin Books 2001; copyright © HIT Entertainment plc, 2001;
text copyright © Katharine Holabird, 1983; illustrations copyright © Helen Craig, 1983
Angelina's Birthday first published by Aurum Press Ltd 1989;
published by Viking and in Puffin Books 2001; copyright © HIT Entertainment plc, 2001;
text copyright © Katharine Holabird, 1989; illustrations copyright © Helen Craig, 1989
Angelina at the Fair first published by Aurum Press Ltd 1985;
published by Viking and in Puffin Books 2001; copyright © HIT Entertainment plc, 2001;
text copyright © Katharine Holabird, 1985; illustrations copyright © Helen Craig, 1985
Angelina's Baby Sister first published by ABC, All Books for Children, a division of The All Children's Company Ltd, 1991;
published by Viking and in Puffin Books 2001; copyright © HIT Entertainment plc, 2001;
text copyright © Katharine Holabird, 1991; illustrations copyright © Helen Craig, 1991
Angelina and the Princess first published by Aurum Press Ltd 1984;
published by Viking and in Puffin Books 2001; copyright © HIT Entertainment plc, 2001;
text copyright © Katharine Holabird, 1984; illustrations copyright © Helen Craig, 1984
Angelina Ice Skates first published by ABC, All Books for Children, a division of The All Children's Company Ltd, 1993;
published by Viking and in Puffin Books 2001; copyright © HIT Entertainment plc, 2001;
text copyright © Katharine Holabird, 1993; illustrations copyright © Helen Craig, 1993

This collection published as *Angelina Ballerina and Other Stories* in Puffin Books 2002
5 7 9 10 8 6 4

Copyright © HIT Entertainment plc, 2001, 2002
Text copyright © Katharine Holabird, 1983, 1989, 1985, 1991, 1984, 1993, 2002
Illustrations copyright © Helen Craig, 1983, 1989, 1985, 1991, 1984, 1993, 2002
Angelina, Angelina Ballerina and the Dancing Angelina logo are trademarks of HIT Entertainment plc,
Katharine Holabird and Helen Craig. Angelina is registered in the UK, Japan and US Pat. & Tm. Off.
The Dancing Angelina logo is registered in the UK.

The moral right of the author and illustrator has been asserted

All rights reserved.
Without limiting the rights under copyright reserved above, no part of this publication may be reproduced, stored in or introduced
into a retrieval system, or transmitted, in any form or by any means (electronic, mechanical, photocopying, recording or otherwise),
without the prior written permission of both the copyright owner and the above publisher of this book

Printed in Singpore

British Library Cataloguing in Publication Data
A CIP catalogue record for this book is available from the British Library

ISBN 0–670–91362–6

This edition produced for The Book People Ltd, Hall Wood Avenue, Haydock, St Helens WA11 9UL.

To find out more about Angelina, visit her web site at **www.angelinaballerina.com**

Angelina Ballerina and Other Stories

Stories by **Katharine Holabird** Illustrations by **Helen Craig**

TED SMART

Angelina Ballerina

More than anything else in the world, Angelina loved to dance. She danced all the time and she danced everywhere, and often she was so busy dancing that she forgot about the other things she was supposed to be doing.

Angelina's mother was always calling to her, "Angelina, it's time to tidy up your room now," or "Please get ready for school now, Angelina." But Angelina never wanted to go to school. She never wanted to do anything but dance.

One night Angelina even danced in her dreams, and
when she woke up in the morning, she knew that
she was going to be a real ballerina some day.

When Mrs Mouseling called Angelina for breakfast,
Angelina was standing on her bed doing curtsies.

When it was time for school, Angelina was trying on her mother's hats and making sad and funny faces at herself in the mirror. "You're going to be late again, Angelina!" cried Mrs Mouseling.

But Angelina did not care. She skipped over rocks

and practised high leaps over the flower-beds until she landed right in old

Mrs Hodgepodge's pansies and got a terrible scolding.

At playtime she twirled and spun across the playground so fast that none of the little boys in her class could catch her and they were all very cross.

After school she did a beautiful arabesque in the kitchen and knocked over a jug of milk and a plate of her mother's best Cheddar cheese pies.

"Oh Angelina, your dancing is nothing but a nuisance!"
exclaimed her mother.

She sent Angelina straight upstairs to her room and went
to have a talk with Mr Mouseling. Mrs Mouseling shook
her head and said, "I just don't know what to do
about Angelina." Mr Mouseling thought awhile and
then he said, "I think I may have an idea."

That same afternoon Mr and Mrs Mouseling
went out together before the shops shut.

The next morning at breakfast Angelina
found a large box with her name on it.

Inside the box was a pink ballet dress and a pair of pink ballet slippers. Angelina's father smiled at her kindly. "I think you are ready to take ballet lessons," he said.

Angelina was so excited that she jumped straight up in the air and landed with one foot in her mother's sewing basket.

The very next day Angelina took her pink slippers and ballet dress and went to her first lesson at Miss Lilly's Ballet School. There were nine other little girls in the class and they all practised curtsies and pliés and ran around the room together just like fairies. Then they skipped and twirled about until it was time to go home.

"Congratulations, Angelina," said Miss Lilly. "You are a good little dancer and if you work hard you may grow up to be a real ballerina one day."

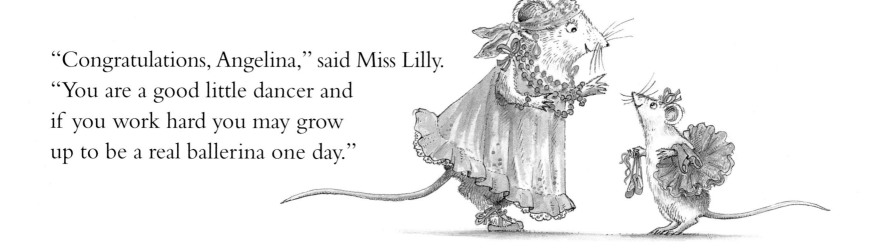

Angelina ran all the way home to give her mother a big hug.
"I'm the happiest little mouse in the world today!" she said.

From that day on, Angelina came downstairs when her mother called her, she tidied her room, and she went to school on time.

She helped her mother
make Cheddar cheese pies

and she even let the boys catch her
in the playground sometimes.

Angelina was so busy dancing at Miss Lilly's that she
didn't need to dance at suppertime or bedtime or on
the way to school any more. She went every day to her
ballet lessons and worked very hard for many years …

… until at last she became the famous ballerina
Mademoiselle Angelina, and people came from
far and wide to enjoy her lovely dancing.

Angelina's Birthday

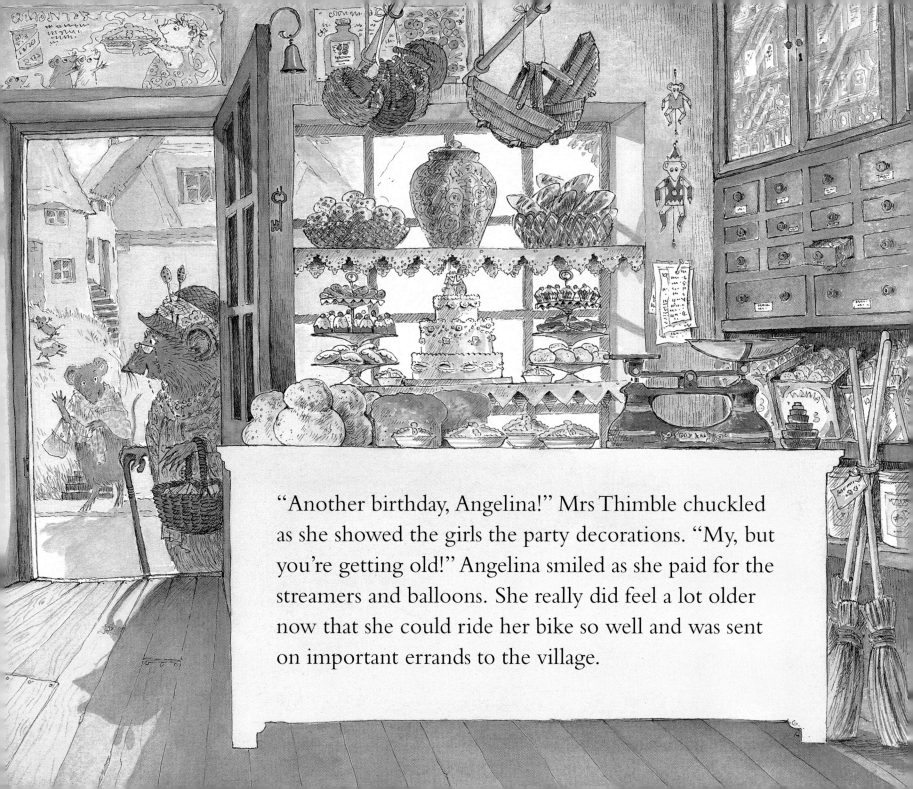

"Another birthday, Angelina!" Mrs Thimble chuckled as she showed the girls the party decorations. "My, but you're getting old!" Angelina smiled as she paid for the streamers and balloons. She really did feel a lot older now that she could ride her bike so well and was sent on important errands to the village.

"Come on, Angelina, let's have a race!" called Alice.

Angelina loved to race Alice down the bumpy road home. "I'll beat you, Alice!" Angelina shouted, going so fast that she didn't see the big rock lying directly in her path.

BANG!

The bike crashed into the rock.
Angelina flew into the air and
then fell to the ground with
a terrible bump.

"OOOOOOOOH! Why did you make me race, Alice!" cried Angelina angrily, pointing to a cut on her foot.

Poor Alice was very upset. She took Angelina's hand and helped her stand up. They looked at the bicycle. One wheel had come off, the other was twisted, and the handlebars were upside down.

"Maybe we can fix it," said Alice.

On Wednesday, Angelina and Alice watered the garden and hung out the washing for Alice's mother, who had a new baby.

On Thursday, they mowed the grass and picked apples for Angelina's grandparents.

On Friday, Angelina and Alice helped Mr Bell, the old postman, repair and paint his front door. Then they walked to Mrs Thimble's store for more balloons.

Angelina was happy. She felt so proud of their hard work and the money they had earned. Then they passed the bicycle shop. There in the window was the most beautiful bicycle Angelina had ever seen. But it was very expensive. Angelina counted all her money. "I haven't even got enough to buy a nice horn for that bike."

"I wish I could buy the bicycle for you," said Alice.

Saturday afternoon was Angelina's birthday party. Alice came early to help blow up the balloons and decorate the garden. Angelina's mother and Aunt Amy had made a delicious picnic, and soon Angelina's friends started arriving.

Flora and Felicity brought Angelina hair ribbons and a book on dancing. Alice gave her a delicate ballerina doll. Cousin Henry gave Angelina a silver horn for when she got another bicycle. Angelina managed to smile and hug Henry, because she knew that he was trying to be kind.

The party games began. The garden filled with singing voices,

"HAPPY BIRTHDAY, ANGELINA!
HAPPY BIRTHDAY TO YOU . . ."

Angelina saw her grandparents, followed by Mrs Hodgepodge, Miss Lilly,
Mrs Thimble, Alice's mother, Mr Bell, and Aunt Amy, all with bicycles!
"We came to have a race with you, Angelina," said her grandmother.

Angelina was surprised. "I'd love to go," she said,
"but I don't have a new bike yet." She felt like crying.

"Angelina! Come and look!" shouted Henry,
who had a terrible time keeping secrets.

And there, hidden behind the garden shed, was the
shiny new bicycle that Angelina and Alice had seen
in the bicycle shop window.

"Oh!" Angelina was so excited she jumped on the bicycle and rode it in circles around and around the garden.

Her grandfather smiled at her and said, "You and Alice worked so hard we all wanted to help buy the bicycle for your birthday."

Then Angelina led everyone on a birthday bicycle
ride over the hills, singing all the way, with
balloons and streamers flying in the wind.

Angelina at the Fair

All winter Angelina had been saving her pocket money for the wonderful day when the fair would come again. When she wasn't busy dancing, she would sit by her window and daydream about the big wheel and the roller coaster. She liked all the most exciting rides.

A big spider dangled just above their heads as they went in ...

and a skeleton jumped out and pointed right at them.

When they bumped into a ghost
Angelina reached out to touch Henry …

but he was gone!

Angelina couldn't see Henry outside the Haunted House either. She ran through the crowds looking for him. She ran past all the rides and all the games, but Henry was nowhere to be found. At last she was so worried and upset that she sat down by the entrance to the fair and began to cry.

And there, watching the balloon man
blow up the beautiful balloons, was
Henry! Angelina was so relieved that
she gave him a big hug and a kiss.
"What is your favourite colour,
Henry?" she asked. Henry chose a
blue balloon.

"What would you like to do now?" Angelina asked kindly.

Henry said he would like to go on the merry-go-round,

so they went on three times and they both loved it.

Afterwards they had a double chocolate ice cream and walked home slowly together. "I like fairs," said Henry, and Angelina smiled.

"You can come with me any time," she said.

Angelina's Baby Sister

Angelina was so excited. Very soon there was going to be a new baby in the family! Angelina couldn't wait to be a big sister, and it was hard to think about anything else — even when Miss Lilly gave Angelina a beautiful china statue as a prize at ballet school.

"Perhaps you can make up a dance to welcome the baby," suggested Miss Lilly when Angelina thanked her. Angelina raced home to show her mother the lovely prize.

Angelina ran so fast that she almost bumped into Dr Tuttle as he was leaving. "Your mother is resting upstairs," he said, "and she has a surprise for you ..."

Angelina leaped up the stairs and into the bedroom – and there were her parents, gazing lovingly at the newborn baby.

"Her name is Polly," said Mrs Mouseling happily. "Would you like to hold her?" Angelina couldn't believe how delicate her little sister was.

"I'll be a good big sister, Polly," Angelina said softly, as she rocked the baby in her arms.

Angelina's father smiled at her. "We know you will," he said.

That evening Angelina and her father made supper while Mrs Mouseling stayed in bed with Polly.

"Don't worry. Pretty soon your mother will be up and around again," said Angelina's father, "but now we have to take good care of her."

Angelina felt sad and confused. Why should
one little baby need so much attention
and make her mother feel so tired?

Angelina played with the pretty china
dancer. Before she went to sleep she
placed it carefully on her chest of
drawers where she could show
it to her mother.

But the next day Angelina's mother was so busy looking
after the new baby that there was no time to look at
Angelina's prize, and the day after that Polly sneezed
several times and Dr Tuttle came back to see that she
didn't catch a cold.

Mr Mouseling was a good cook, but Angelina
missed her mother's special Cheddar cheese
pies after school. Having a baby sister
was not at all the way Angelina
had imagined it would be!

A whole week went by. Angelina
went to school every day and
tried to be good while
everyone fussed over
Polly, but it was
very hard.

The weekend came, and
could hardly wait to see
answer it. "Gra

A

Angelina grabbed one of her stuffed toys and threw it as hard as she could across the room, where it landed with a thud. Then she threw another and another. Angelina threw all of her stuffed toys and all of her dolls. Then she threw all her paper and crayons. She jumped up and down on her bed and she gave her chest of drawers a terrific kick. The chest of drawers shook, and down fell the china dancer, where it broke on the floor and lay in pieces.

Mrs Mouseling had baked Angelina's favourite Cheddar cheese pies. "I wanted to surprise you," she said.

Then Mr Mouseling played his fiddle and Angelina did her special dance to welcome her baby sister, while Polly giggled with delight.

That night, Angelina showed Polly her favourite book, and helped put her to bed. "You know," she whispered, "when you get bigger I'm going to teach you to dance too!"

Angelina and the Princess

Angelina was much too excited to sleep. The students at Miss Lilly's Ballet School had been asked to dance for Her Royal Highness, the Princess of Mouseland. Mr Lightfoot, Director of the famous Royal Ballet Company, was coming tomorrow to help Miss Lilly choose the best ballerinas for the special performance. Angelina wanted a leading part so much that she worked on her pliés and pirouettes far into the night when she should have been sound asleep.

The next morning Angelina woke up feeling terrible. Her head ached and her ears buzzed. Angelina's mother took her temperature and shook her head sadly. "I'm afraid you'll have to stay in bed," she said. "You can't go to ballet school when you're not well."

But Angelina was determined to go. While her mother was busy downstairs Angelina packed her ballet bag …

… and tiptoed out of the house.

Angelina arrived at Miss Lilly's Ballet School just in time to join her friends Flora and Felicity and all the other ballerinas who were waiting to go on stage. Flora did a nimble leap and a delicate spin …

… and then it was Angelina's turn to dance. Her heart started beating like a drum and she couldn't remember what she was supposed to be doing.

… then she began twirling and spinning like a top until she was so dizzy she lost her balance, tripped on her pink ribbons and tumbled down with a thump.

Flora and Felicity were given the leading roles in the Dance of the Flower Fairies. Later, Miss Lilly called for Angelina. "I'm afraid you will have to take a smaller part this time," she said, trying to be kind.

When Angelina got home her mother was very upset.
"How could you run away like that when I told you to
stay in bed?" she asked.

Angelina burst into tears. "I had to go to Miss Lilly's, but everything went wrong. I danced so badly for Mr Lightfoot I will never be a real ballerina. I am not going to ballet school any more."

Angelina's mother hugged her and kissed her and
carried her upstairs, and in just a minute she was
fast asleep in her own bed again.

The next day Angelina's headache was gone.
She felt better, but she was still very sad.
"It's not fair!" said Angelina.

"Maybe not," her mother said gently, "but things don't always go our way. You can still do your best with whatever part you are given, and that will help the whole performance."

Angelina thought about what her mother had said. Then she returned to Miss Lilly's after all, and rehearsed very hard with the other ballerinas for the Royal Performance.

After she had learned her own part, she memorized
the Dance of the Flower Fairies while watching
Flora and Felicity.

On the day of the Royal Performance, just as the show
was about to begin, Flora tripped and sprained her ankle.
Everyone was terribly upset.

Mr Lightfoot and Miss Lilly turned to each other in horror. "Who can do the part?" they cried. Angelina was worried about Flora, but Susie stepped forward and said, "Angelina can!"

Angelina showed Miss Lilly that she had learned the dance by heart. "But what about Flora?" she asked.

"Don't worry," said Miss Lilly, "we have a treat for her …"

… So Flora was happy because she was invited to sit right next to the Princess of Mouseland. Mr Lightfoot and Miss Lilly were happy because the performance could go on. Angelina was happy because she did the Dance of the Flower Fairies without forgetting a single step. The Princess of Mouseland was happy because she loved ballet.

When the performance was over she congratulated Angelina and thanked her warmly for saving the show.

Angelina Ice Skates

Angelina absolutely loved snowy winter days when she could ice skate with her friends on Miller's Pond. The ice sparkled like glass and they raced across it in pairs, practising spins and twirls and figure-eights.

Everyone in the village was getting ready for New Year's Eve, and Angelina was preparing a special ice skating show. Her little cousin Henry wanted to be in the show, too, even though he often tumbled off the ice and fell into the snowbanks.

"We'll need someone to be the Snow King," said Angelina's friend Flora, pirouetting across the ice as the Snow Princess.

"I'll be the King!" shouted Henry, but then he tripped and slid into Alice, who was going to be the Snow Fairy.

"You'd be a better snow shovel!" said Alice crossly as she dusted off her skates.

"Don't worry, Henry," said Angelina. "Hold on to me and let's practise skating together."

They linked their tails and tried to skate in a circle, but it wasn't easy on the slippery ice. Just then Spike and Sammy, two big boys from school, raced by playing hockey and almost knocked them all over.

"HEY!" shouted Felicity, but the boys were already gone, laughing and yelling across the ice.

"Never mind," said Angelina, helping Felicity get her balance. "Let me show you how to skate backwards."

But, before long, Spike and Sammy tore past again, spraying snow in all directions. When they zipped through Angelina's rehearsal a third time, she got angry.

"Please stop interrupting us!" she scolded.

But the boys just laughed, grabbed Angelina's scarf, and tweaked Flora's whiskers.

"Little ballerinas can't catch us!" they shouted as they zoomed away.

Angelina and her friends chased Spike and Sammy all across the ice, and then Angelina made a huge snowball and hurled it at the boys.

"Great! A snowball fight!" Spike yelled, throwing one back at Angelina. Then everybody started throwing snowballs everywhere, and soon Miller's Pond was a blizzard of flying snow and shouting skaters.

They had so much fun, they stayed until Flora got ice down her neck and Alice's toes began to freeze. Then they trudged back to Angelina's house, feeling tired and frozen.

"What's wrong?" asked Angelina's mother.

"Our New Year's Eve Ice Dance is a mess," said Angelina sadly. "We haven't got costumes or scenery and Spike and Sammy keep bothering us."

"I can help you with costumes," said Mrs Mouseling. "And maybe the boys are teasing you because they want you to pay attention to them."

Angelina was surprised. "That gives me an idea."

The next day Angelina put on her skates and whizzed past Spike and Sammy, snatched their caps, and raced off laughing with the boys just behind her. They were very fast, but Angelina could do all sorts of tricky twists and spins and, just as Spike and Sammy thought they would grab her, she spun out of reach and they smashed into each other, collapsing on the ice.

Spike gazed at Angelina in admiration.
"You ballerinas are fast!"

"Would you like to be in our show?"
asked Angelina, tossing back their caps.

Spike and Sammy leaped up. "Yes!"
they shouted, skating in circles around her.

On New Year's Eve, the whole village dressed up and
came to celebrate. Miller's Pond looked magical as the

performers skated on to the ice in Mrs Mouseling's costumes,
and Henry's snow fort gleamed in the moonlight.

When Angelina danced into the spotlight that night, she felt just like a real snow queen. Spike and Sammy did exciting leaps and jumps together and Henry was thrilled to be the King's attendant, while Felicity, Flora, and Alice seemed to fly across the ice like delicate snowflakes.

At the end of the performance, as the magic hour
of midnight approached and fireworks sparkled in
the sky, Angelina and her friends wished everyone
joy and peace, and they all sang and danced
together to welcome in the New Year.